D0583138

CONTENTS

When the champions of Earth came together to battle a threat too big for a single hero, they realized the value of strength in numbers. Together they formed an unstoppable team, dedicated to defending the planet from the forces of evil. They are the . . .

{ MEMBERS }

THE FLASH

CYBORG

SUPERMAN

WONDER WOMAN

BATMAN

GREEN
LANTERN
(HAL JORDAN)

AQUAMAN

MARTIAN
MANHUNTER

HAWKGIRL

HAWKMAN

GREEN ARROW

BLACK CANARY

GREEN LANTERN
(JOHN STEWART)

THE ATOM

SUPERGIRL

RED TORNADO

POWER GIRL

SHAZAM

PLASTIC MAN

BOOSTER GOLD

BLUE BEETLE

ZATANNA

VIXEN

METAMORPHO

ETRIGAN
THE DEMON

FIRESTORM

HUNTRESS

CHAPTER 1

SURPRISE GUEST

"Are you ready, Supergirl?" asked Superman. His voice echoed through the cold, empty chamber.

"Bring it on," Supergirl answered.

It was training day in the Watchtower's state-of-the-art Fight Room as the Girl of Steel prepared for battle. She was eager to show her Kryptonian cousin that she had what it took to become a full-time Justice League member. Supergirl had worked with the team countless times, but she had never been offered a full-time position.

After some arm-twisting, Superman gave her a chance to prove herself worthy. She'd face off against a series of holograms so the team could measure her skills and abilities.

Get your head in the game, Kara, she thought. *Show them that you're ready to commit to the Justice League one hundred per cent.*

With the press of a button, the Fight Room changed into a lush Kryptonian jungle filled with alien plants. Superman and Batman watched remotely from the Watchtower's control centre as Supergirl braced for battle.

STOMP! STOMP! STOMP!

An enormous Octosaur appeared from the brush. It was a scaly Kryptonian beast with slimy tentacles and webbed dinosaur feet. As it lurched towards Supergirl, she launched herself into the air to avoid the attack.

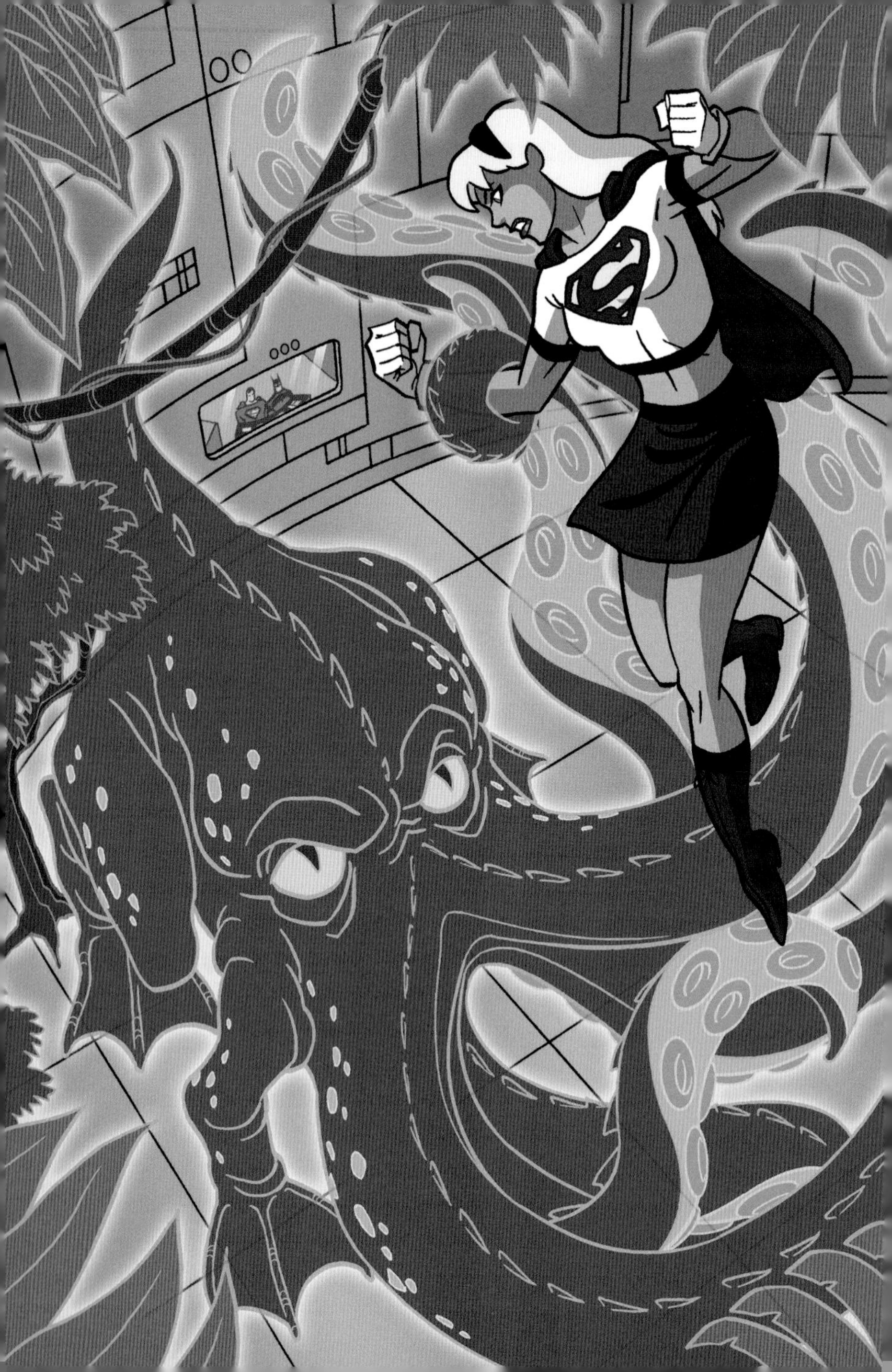

"Is this supposed to *hurt* me?" she asked. "C'mon, guys. You'll have to do better than some old monster." Supergirl grabbed the Octosaur's tentacles, tied them in a knot and threw the beast away with ease. "Have you got a *real* challenge?" she taunted.

Batman was impressed. "She's got spirit," he said.

"Could be luck," said Superman. "How about we try something new?" He pressed a button. A pair of glowing red eyes lit up inside a nearby cave. They stared at Supergirl, watching her every move. In an instant, the serpentine Drang slithered out and thrust its horned head in her direction.

ROAR!

The creature bared its sharp fangs. It snapped them in Supergirl's direction, causing her to flinch.

"Those are some nice chompers you've got there," Supergirl said as she grabbed the Drang's jaw to keep it from closing on her. "For a hologram, your breath sure *stinks*."

Supergirl thrust herself from the Drang's deadly grip and circled him at super speed. As the beast grew dizzier, she smacked it in the snout, causing it to pass out.

"Are we finished yet, Superman?" Supergirl asked. "I'm getting hungry."

Wonder Woman joined Superman and Batman in the control centre. "That was a crafty bit of strategy. Why haven't we offered Supergirl *full-time* membership?" she asked.

"It's complicated," Superman replied.

"Not from what I see," said Wonder Woman. "Supergirl has taken part in countless Justice League missions. She's more than qualified to serve alongside us."

Superman wasn't convinced. "You haven't known her as long as I have. She's restless and impatient," he replied. "She could do with a little more training."

Superman pressed another button and a chamber opened to reveal one of Krypton's most dangerous creatures: the Torquat. It had a mane of spiky purple quills that ran down its back and clawed paws it used to tear apart its prey.

GROWL!

The ferocious Torquat startled Supergirl as it stalked her from behind. She turned to find the creature bearing its razor-like teeth. "Easy, big fella," she said. "Be a nice boy."

In an instant, the Torquat pounced on top of Supergirl and pinned her to the ground. She delivered a swift kick to its underbelly, which sent the beast flying into the jungle.

Supergirl proudly rose to her feet. "That was *easy*," she said with a smile.

The Torquat hadn't finished with Supergirl just yet. He bounded from the trees at lightning speed, heading straight for her.

"Kara, look out!" Superman shouted.

SMACK! Supergirl turned just in time to punch the creature square in the jaw. It fell to the ground with a **THUD!**

The jungle landscape faded away, returning the Fight Room to its original state. Supergirl cheerfully greeted Superman, Wonder Woman and Batman as they entered the room. "How did I do?" she asked.

Superman hesitated to answer, choosing his words carefully. "You can't just kick away a Torquat and assume it is beaten. It's one of Krypton's most dangerous predators."

"I know what a Torquat is, Superman. I grew up with them, remember?" Supergirl said, dusting herself off.

"Yes, but your carelessness will get you hurt," Superman warned. "Being a member of the Justice League isn't a game, Kara."

Supergirl grew frustrated. "I'm not a little girl, and I'm just as powerful as *you*," she reminded him. "I appreciate the workout, but I'm not sure why I have to prove myself."

"You keep relying on your super-strength to win. You need to develop your other abilities," said Superman. "You've still got a lot to learn."

Supergirl's anger boiled over. "I've put *tonnes* of time and energy into developing my powers! This whole training session is a joke!" she scoffed. "Sometimes I wish I'd never even come to Earth in the first place."

CRASH! The Watchtower shook with violent fury. "What was that?!" asked Wonder Woman.

Superman used his X-ray vision to scan for danger. "Some sort of strange spacecraft has punctured the Watchtower's lower level," he said. "We've got to get down there before the Watchtower loses air pressure."

As the heroes raced to prevent their headquarters from falling towards Earth, a familiar green glow skyrocketed onto the scene. Green Lantern had arrived after a journey in deep space. He used his emerald ring to gather metal debris floating in space. Then he used them to patch the breach.

"*That* should do it," Green Lantern said, inspecting his work. "Now to move this spaceship into the shuttle bay to have a better look."

Superman, Wonder Woman, Batman and Supergirl greeted Green Lantern as he brought the odd-looking ship in for closer inspection.

"Thanks for that, Green Lantern," Superman said.

"Not a problem. I was in the area. Any idea where *this* came from?" Green Lantern said as he studied the craft. It was a strange patchwork of metals, crudely melted together. A broken antenna stuck out of the top.

"It wasn't built by someone who knew what they were doing," said Batman.

"What do you think is inside?" asked Supergirl.

Superman scanned the ship with his X-ray vision. "I know *exactly* what's inside," he said, ripping off the ship's cockpit to reveal a surprise. "*Bizarro!*"

The dim duplicate, with a rocky #1 medallion hanging around his neck, sat in a slump. He had passed out during the collision with the Watchtower.

"Uggghhh," Bizarro groaned, struggling to wake up.

Superman grabbed him by the collar and threw him out of the ship. "What do you think you're doing, Bizarro?" he growled. "You put us all in danger!"

"Be careful, Superman," Batman warned.

Bizarro lunged towards Superman, gripping him by the shoulders. "Superman not understand!" he shouted.

"I understand perfectly. You want to cause trouble *as usual*," Superman said. The Man of Steel pushed Bizarro away and threw him against the wall.

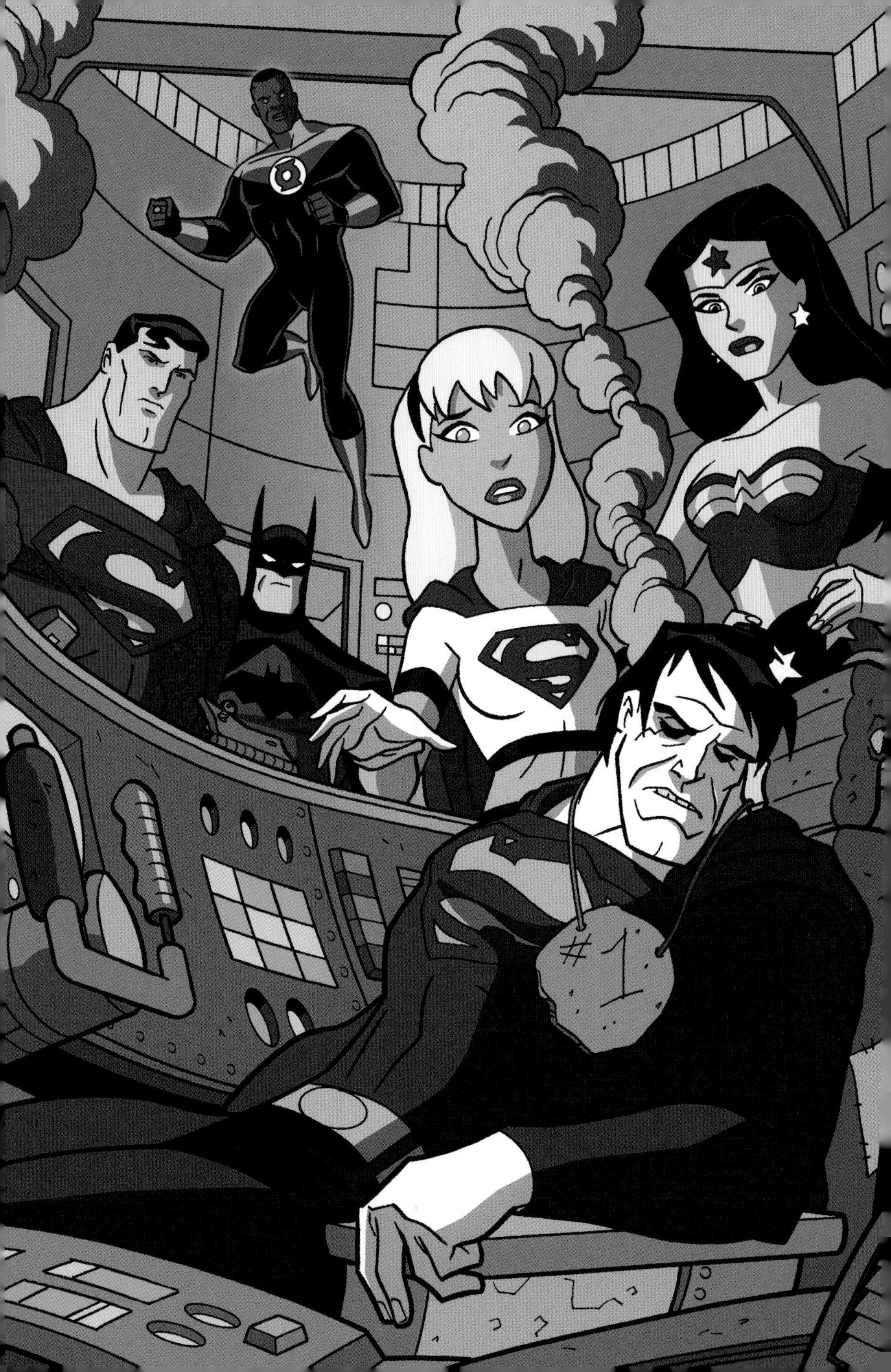
#1

Bizarro shook off the shove and charged towards Superman, throwing wild punches in every direction. The Man of Steel sidestepped each one. The confused clone couldn't land a single blow.

"Superman not listen!" Bizarro barked. "You make Bizarro *so mad!*"

Superman and Bizarro blasted each other with heat and freeze vision at the exact same time. The room filled with blinding red and white light as the two rivals battled it out.

Batman had seen enough. It was clear to him this wasn't an ordinary visit. He switched on his cowl's voice amplifying device to end the fight.

"*STOP!*" the Dark Knight shouted. The booming sound caused Superman and Bizarro to separate.

"Enough bickering you two," roared Wonder Woman.

Bizarro sniffled, wiping away a small tear that had formed in the corner of his eye. Something troubled him.

"Is he *crying?*" Supergirl whispered.

Bizarro took a deep breath. "Me come from very far away for important mission," the villain explained, his voice cracking. "Something very bad happening and Bizarro need Justice League to help. Please help Bizarro, Justice League."

The heroes looked at one another in disbelief. They weren't quite sure what to do.

"Start at the beginning, Bizarro," Batman said. "Don't leave anything out."

CHAPTER 2

TROUBLE AT HOME

"Okay, Bizarro. Let's go over this one more time," Green Lantern said, pacing back and forth. It had been more than an hour since Bizarro crashed his ship into the Watchtower. Since then he'd told his story a handful of times, but his strange, broken language wasn't easy to understand. The Justice League struggled to piece together the truth.

"Are you telling us that Lex Luthor gave *you* the same cloning technology he used to make you?" asked Green Lantern.

"That am true," Bizarro replied.

"But that doesn't make any sense," replied Green Lantern.

"I'm not an expert in Bizarro speak," Supergirl interrupted. "But I think he said that Luthor's exact words were 'You're annoying me, you broken, stupid thing! Take this useless junk back to your miserable little planet and make some new friends. Leave me alone!'"

Green Lantern looked at Bizarro. "Is *that* what Luthor said?" he asked.

"That am what he said!" the villain exclaimed with a smile. "Me make other Bizarros but then they take over world and kick first Bizarro out. Me no like! Me need Justice League to help kick bad Bizarros out and take planet back!"

"Why would Luthor give Bizarro his cloning technology?" Superman asked.

"I suspect Luthor didn't think Bizarro would get the device to work," said Batman. "But he's smarter than Luthor thought."

"Bizarro am no dummy!" he cheered.

"Of course you aren't, big guy," said Supergirl, gently patting Bizarro on the back. This show of affection calmed the clone.

"Supergirl, take Bizarro to the dining area," said Batman. "The rest of us need to discuss a few things in private."

"Oh, um, okay," Supergirl said. "C'mon, Bizarro. Let's grab a bite to eat. I'm *starving*."

Superman looked concerned as Supergirl and Bizarro left the room together. "Are you sure that's a good idea?" he asked.

"He likes her. She has a calming effect on him," said Batman. "We'll watch the monitor to make sure nothing happens."

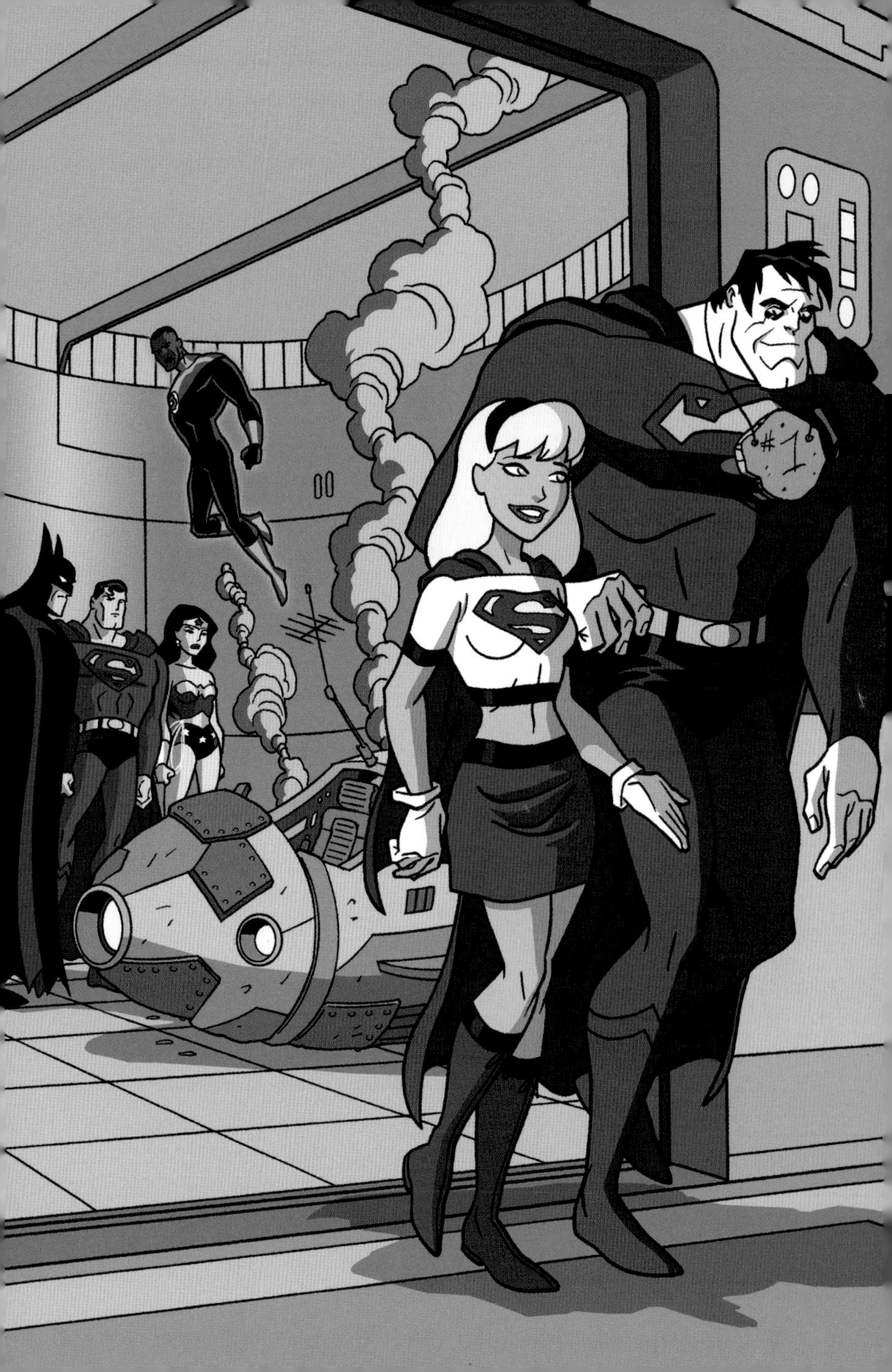
#1

Wonder Woman was restless. "Our mission is clear, is it not? We need to go to Bizarro's world and stop these out of control clones," she said firmly.

"You can't be serious," said Green Lantern. "Bizarro has tried to take us down so many times before. This is probably some kind of trap. Why should we help *him?*"

"Bizarro is unpredictable, but he's not evil. There's *good* in him. I know that much for sure," Superman explained. "If he came here looking for help, it means he's desperate. *That* worries me more than anything."

"Agreed," said Wonder Woman. "His behaviour has always been influenced by those that surround him. Positive role models change his behaviour for the better."

"That's true," Batman said. "His responses are like a child's."

"I don't know," said Green Lantern. "The whole situation seems nutty."

"Bizarro and I share a bond. He was made using my DNA. My genetic material is part of who he is. I feel responsible for him," Superman said. "He's got a temper, but he responds to kindness."

"*You* didn't show him much kindness when you yanked him out of that spaceship," Batman said.

"I apologize for that. I jumped to conclusions," replied Superman. "I should have looked at the situation more carefully before acting."

A sly smile appeared on Batman's face. "Perhaps you need a little more *training?*" he suggested. "Nevertheless, the three of you need to go to Bizarro's world, find out what's happening, and put a stop to it."

"You're not going to join us?" Superman asked.

"I'm not made for deep space travel," Batman said. "But don't worry, I won't leave you without a little insurance." He pulled a small metal box out of his Utility Belt.

"What's this?" Superman asked, scanning the box with his X-ray vision.

"A little something I prepared in case of an emergency. You might find it helpful," Batman explained.

"It's lead-lined. I can't see inside. That's *not* a good sign," said Superman.

"The clones Bizarro created using Luthor's flawed tech are probably more unpredictable than the original. If the situation gets out of hand, you'll thank me for giving you that," said Batman. "Use it wisely."

* * *

In the dining area, Supergirl watched as
Bizarro wolfed down two bags of crisps in
ten seconds flat. He flung his head back and
released a loud belch. **BUUURP!**

Supergirl tried not to giggle. She wasn't
quite sure how to handle Bizarro. She'd heard
the stories of his mischief and mayhem. *He
seems harmless,* she thought. *But Superman
told me he gets angry easily. I've got to be
careful not to make him upset.*

Supergirl tried some awkward small talk.
"I'm sorry your other Bizarro pals turned on
you," she said.

"Other Bizarros not pals. They enemies!"
Bizarro said, smashing his fist into the table.
"They supposed to keep Bizarro company, but
then they turn rude. Me no like rude people!"

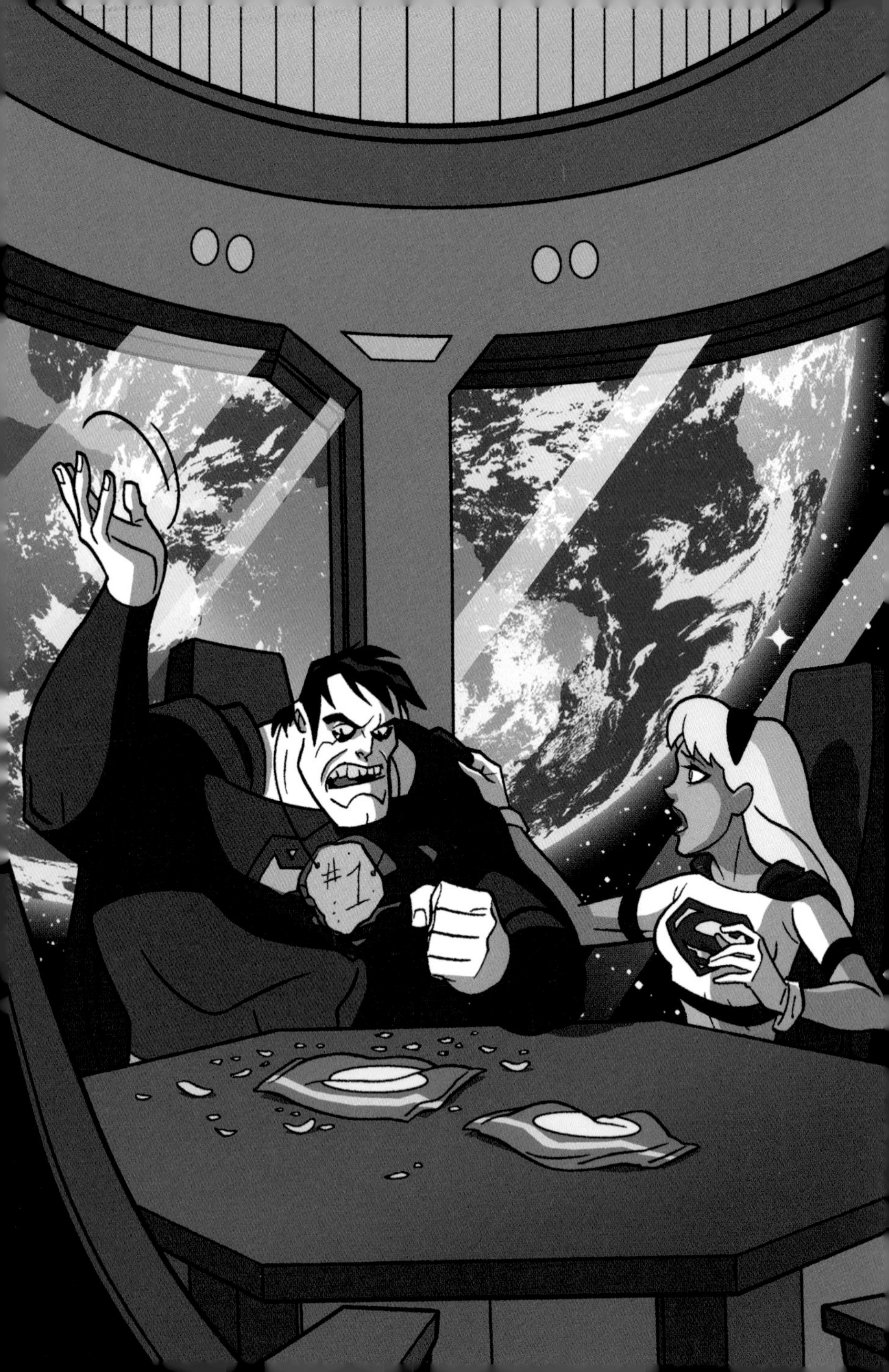
#1

"I hear you on that one," Supergirl agreed.

"They took Bizarro's very best friend, Bizarro-Krypto! He the most important thing in Bizarro's life. Me going to find those bad Bizarros and make them pay," he growled.

Bizarro's anger and random behaviour made Supergirl nervous, but she did her best to appear calm. "I know what it's like to lose someone you care about," she said. "I'm lucky I have family like Superman, even though he can be annoying sometimes."

"Superman am Bizarro's family!" Bizarro exclaimed, pointing to himself. "Will Supergirl be Bizarro's family *too?*"

"Well, yes, I suppose so," said Supergirl. Bizarro's face broke out into a smile. He grabbed Supergirl and excitedly hugged her.

"Not so tight," she whispered.

Superman, Wonder Woman and Green Lantern entered the dining area. They were shocked to find Bizarro being so affectionate.

"All right, Bizarro," said Superman. "We'll take you home and help you stop these other Bizarros. I expect you to behave yourself."

Bizarro jumped up and down like an anxious child. "Supergirl am Bizarro's family!" he exclaimed. "She come too!"

"Supergirl won't be joining us," Superman declared.

"No!" Bizarro said, stomping his feet. "She come *or else.*"

Supergirl put her hand on Bizarro's back to calm him. "It's okay. You'll be fine without me," she said. "Superman will help you rescue Bizarro-Krypto."

"There's a Bizarro version of your dog?!" Green Lantern asked Superman. "This just gets weirder and weirder."

"Bad Bizarros *took* Bizarro-Krypto. Me need to get him back!" exclaimed Bizarro. "Supergirl help find Bizarro's best friend."

"She *does* have a positive effect on him," Wonder Woman said. "We could use someone who can keep Bizarro in check."

"That's a pretty tall order," said Supergirl. "I promise to do my best."

"Fine," Superman said. "But we don't know what's waiting for us on Bizarro's world. Things might get dangerous quickly. Stay focused and follow orders."

"You got it." Supergirl nodded. She wasn't sure what she was getting herself into but was thrilled to be a part of the adventure.

"Bizarro's home planet is far away," Green Lantern said. "We should get going."

Superman, Wonder Woman, Green Lantern, Supergirl and Bizarro boarded the Javelin and blasted into space. To pass the time, Supergirl studied the most powerful villains in the Justice League's database.

Wonder Woman was impressed by her desire to learn. "You're a smart young lady who's shown a lot of promise," she said. "Be patient, Supergirl. Great things await you."

"Thank you, Wonder Woman," Supergirl said. "Can I ask you something?"

"Of course," Wonder Woman replied.

"Is my cousin angry with me? Sometimes he treats me like I'm still a kid. I know he just wants to protect me, but I'm *not* a baby. I'm a *super hero*," Supergirl explained.

Wonder Woman thought for a moment, then chose her words carefully. "You *are* a super hero. Superman sees that. He believes in you as we all do," she explained. "But the world is a dangerous place. Superman just wants to make sure you're protected."

* * *

In the ship's cockpit, Bizarro had perched himself between Superman and Green Lantern. He was growing more and more restless. "Are we at Bizarro's home yet?" he asked.

"*No.* Just like I told you the last ten times you asked," said Green Lantern.

"I'm proud of you, Bizarro," said Superman. "You've been pretty calm for the entire trip. I know that's not the easiest thing for you to do."

"Me just want to go home and find Bizarro-Krypto," Bizarro said with a tiny whimper.

"I know you do," said Superman. "We'll find him. I promise."

Bizarro's peaceful mood soon disappeared. "Monster!" he shouted, pointing towards a giant tentacled beast that had appeared in the Javelin's path. The imposing creature was bright green, covered in scales and had a single red eye.

"Everyone brace yourselves!" exclaimed Green Lantern. "This ride is about to get a little bumpy."

CHAPTER 3

DANGER IN SPACE

CREECH!

The massive creature cried out in anger, slapping the Javelin away with its electrified tentacles. Green Lantern fired the ship's laser cannons, but the giant space monster shook off the attack.

"What is that thing?" asked Superman.

"I don't know," answered Green Lantern. "This sector is mostly empty."

"It looks like a big, green beach ball with spaghetti legs," Supergirl said.

"The beast could be lost and frightened. That would explain why it's lashing out," said Wonder Woman.

"Good thinking," Superman said. "If that's the case, we don't want to make the situation worse by doing anything reckless."

The monster's giant eye glowed bright red.

"It's about to attack again!" shrieked Supergirl.

ZAP! A burst of strange energy fried the Javelin's circuitry, causing it to burst into flames. Superman used his freeze-breath to put the fire out.

CREECH! One of the beast's tentacles wrapped around the Javelin's wing, crushing it like a piece of foil. Before the heroes could act, Bizarro appeared outside the ship, pounding on the monster's enormous body.

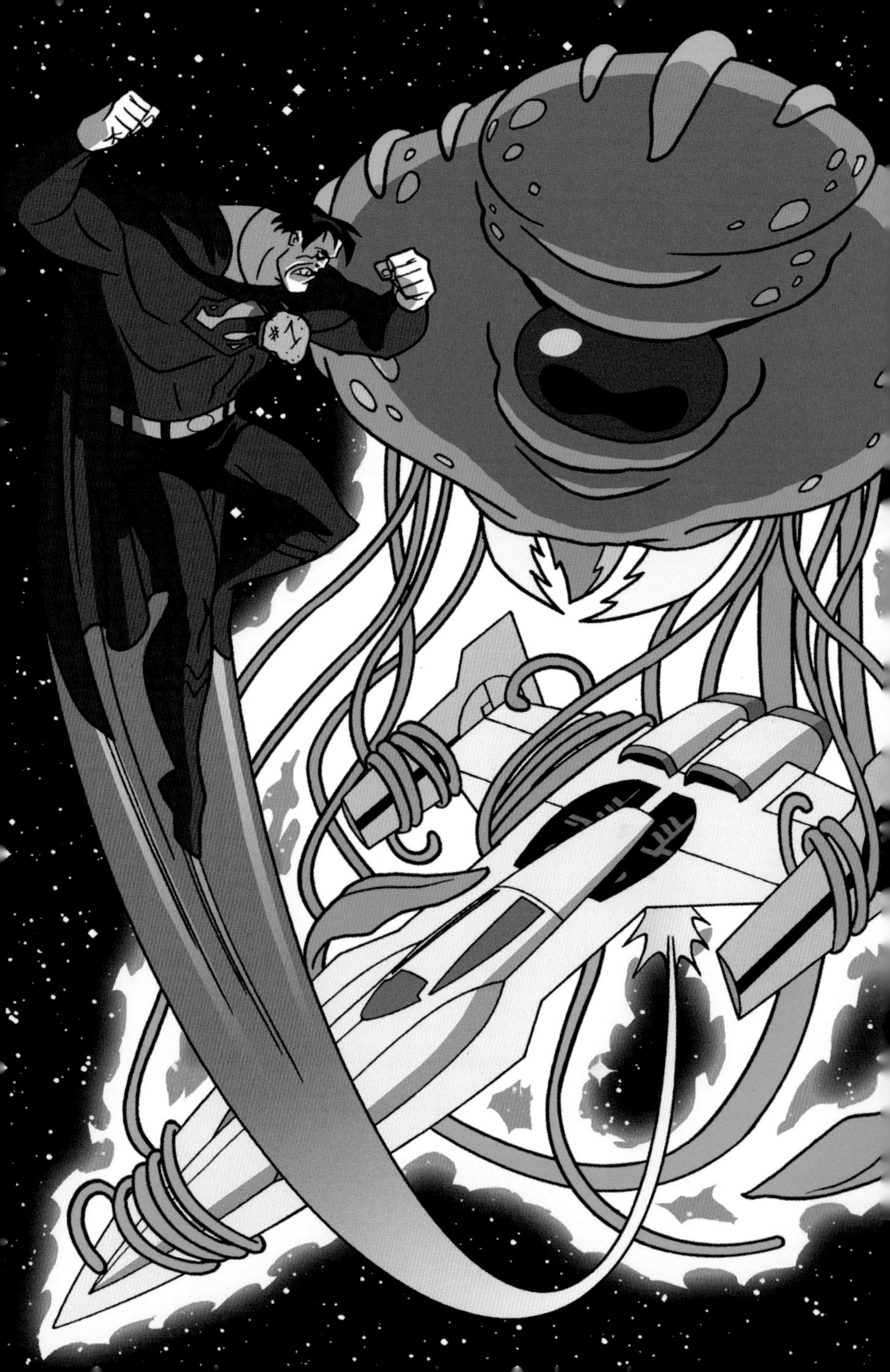

"You stop now!" Bizarro shouted.

"How did he get out there?" exclaimed Green Lantern.

"That little sneak," whispered Supergirl.

The creature became annoyed with Bizarro's pestering. It used its tentacles to swat him away like an insect, shattering his rocky medallion. That made Bizarro angry.

"Leave my friends alone!" Bizarro shouted. He tried to pry the creature from the Javelin, but its grasp was too tight.

Thankfully, Superman swooped in and used his heat vision to sear the Javelin's thermal shield. It became so hot the beast released its grip. Then the Man of Steel remembered how Supergirl defeated the holographic Octosaur. He tied the creature's tentacles in a knot and flung it into space.

"Bye-bye, spaghetti legs!" Bizarro cheered.

The incident was over, but Superman wasn't happy with Bizarro taking matters into his own hands. "Don't do that again, Bizarro. You could have got us all hurt," he growled.

"Me only wanted to help," Bizarro said, defeated.

Inside the Javelin's cockpit, Green Lantern checked for damage. "That thing really hurt the ship. It desperately needs repair," he explained.

Wonder Woman brought up a star map on screen. "There's a small, empty planet nearby," she said. "We'll land there and regroup."

"Sounds like a plan," Green Lantern said, charting a course.

Supergirl noticed Bizarro moping in the corner and went to comfort him. "Hey, big guy. Thanks for what you did," she said. "Now we've got something else in common. Superman gets angry with me too."

"But why?" asked Bizarro. "Supergirl am hero."

"He's just being protective," Supergirl explained. "And maybe a little controlling. Don't let it get to you."

Soon the Javelin landed on a planet littered with bottomless craters and rocky ridges. Everyone but Bizarro got out to check the ship's damage. Superman grounded him for acting without thinking.

"It's not as bad as I suspected, but it'll take time to repair," Green Lantern said, reviewing the ship's damage. "Superman, Wonder Woman, I could use your help."

"You got it," Superman said.

"What about me?" asked Supergirl. "I'm pretty good with a spanner."

"Thanks for the offer, but we can handle it," Green Lantern said.

Supergirl let out a long sigh. "I'll just sit this one out, I suppose. Even though I have all the same powers as my cousin. Seems like a total waste but *whatever*," she said under her breath.

"Stay close," Superman said. "This won't take long."

As Green Lantern, Superman and Wonder Woman began their work, Supergirl spotted a unique rock formation in the distance. *Cool,* she thought, *no one will notice if I sneak away for one quick second. What's a trip through space without a little souvenir to take home?*

Bizarro watched from the Javelin's cockpit window as Supergirl took off into the sky. He wished he could join her but was careful not to disobey Superman's orders.

"Wow," Supergirl said, arriving at the rock formation. "How *beautiful.*" The rocky structure was stark white and looked like the crest of a giant ocean wave. A sprinkling of mineral dust covered the area, making it sparkle in the moonlight.

Supergirl found a disc-shaped piece of rock that had fallen from the formation. She used her heat vision to carve the number one onto it as a gift for Bizarro. *Maybe this will cheer him up,* she thought.

RUMBLE! A tremor shook the ground underneath Supergirl's feet. Before she knew it, a jagged hand reached up from the depths and grabbed her by the ankles.

A hulking rock beast, ten storeys high, rose from the ground below. He gripped Supergirl tightly, studying her as if she was an insect. The cranky rock creature's body was made of random-sized boulders and other assorted pieces of rubble.

"Ahhh!" Supergirl screamed.

Bizarro's super-hearing picked up her cries. In an instant he zoomed out of the Javelin, past the working heroes.

"I'll get him," said Green Lantern, taking off in Bizarro's direction.

Bizarro arrived to find Supergirl struggling to free herself. He tried prying her from the monster's grasp, but it was no use.

"Let Bizarro's family go!" he screamed. The rock beast laughed in his face then kicked him into the sky.

Luckily, Green Lantern was there to help. He caught Bizarro and set him safely on the ground.

"Stay out of this," Green Lantern warned. He then turned his attention to the rock creature. "Brace yourself, Supergirl."

Using his ring, Green Lantern created a giant baseball bat, which he used to smash the creature to pieces, freeing Supergirl in the process. "They don't call baseball America's favourite pastime for nothing," he laughed.

"Thanks, Green Lantern," said Supergirl.

Bizarro tapped Green Lantern on the shoulder and pointed behind him. The battle wasn't over yet. The rock monster had swiftly reformed. This time it was bigger and angrier than before.

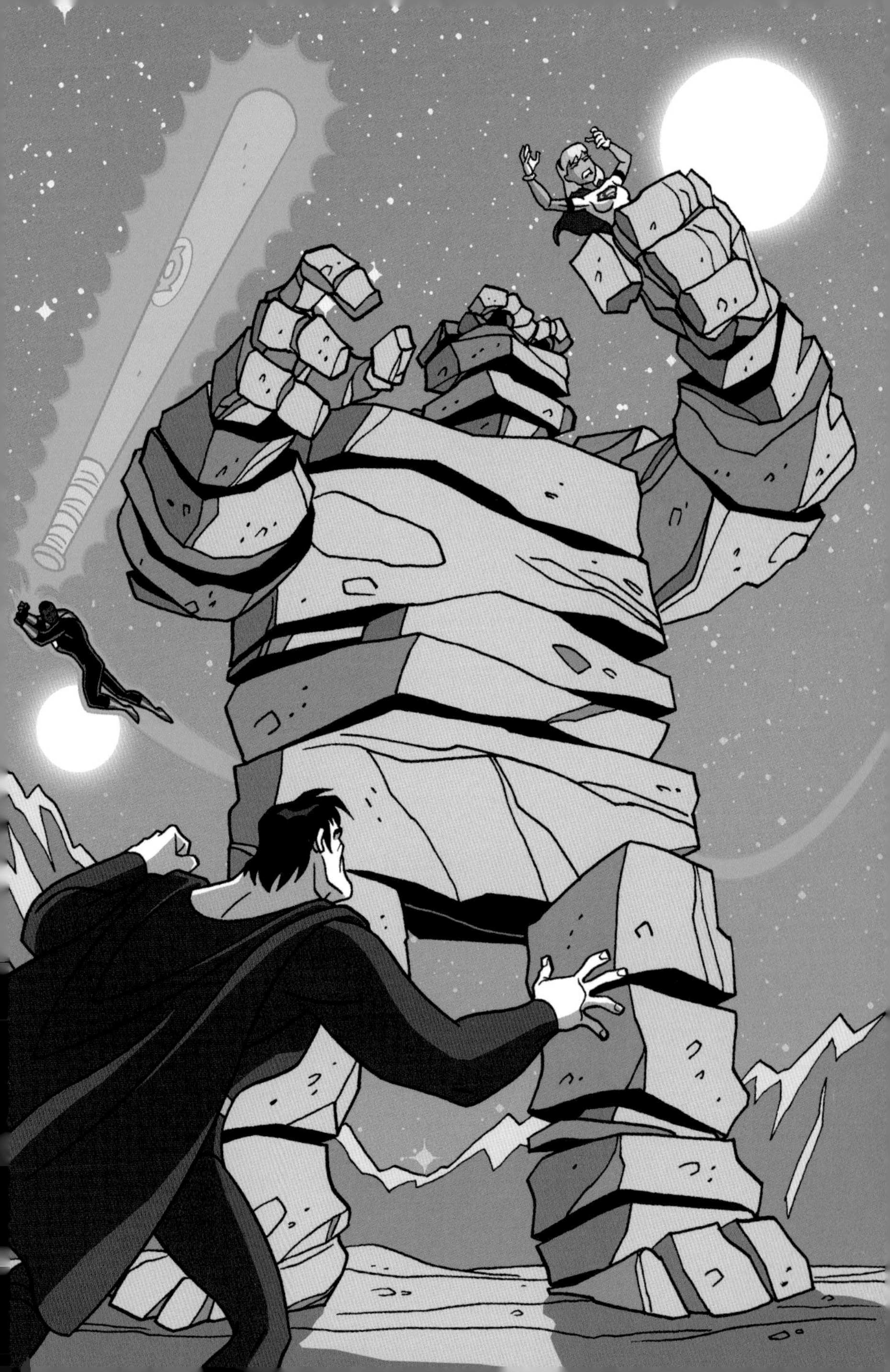

"Do you want to play?" Green Lantern asked as a suit of glowing green armour covered his body. "Let's see what you've got!"

The Emerald Knight raised his sword into the air and swatted the rock creature. Soon it was scattered on the ground, completely broken apart.

Supergirl was embarrassed that Green Lantern had had to save her. "You're not going to tell my cousin about this, right?" she asked.

"He already knows," Superman said, surprising her from behind.

"I just wanted to look around," Supergirl said. "I didn't expect *this* to happen."

"I told you to stay close, yet you thought it would be a good idea to *sneak off?* What's got into you, Kara?" Superman exclaimed.

"Sneaking?! I wanted to *explore,* that's all," said Supergirl. "We're in the middle of space. I didn't think some crazy rock monster would pop up out of nowhere."

"That's exactly right. You didn't *think,*" Superman said.

"Leave Supergirl alone," Bizarro growled. He was fiercely protective of the young hero and didn't like Superman's harsh tone. "She only want to *explore.*"

"Go back to the ship, Bizarro!" Superman exclaimed. "This doesn't concern you."

"You not tell Bizarro what to do anymore!" he screamed, shaking his fist in Superman's direction. Bizarro wanted to strike him, but he knew it was the wrong thing to do. "Take Bizarro to his home, then *leave.* Me no want to be around you anymore."

Shaking with rage, Bizarro sat down on the ground to calm himself. Supergirl walked over and handed him the disc-shaped piece of rock she'd found.

"I made this for you," Supergirl said. "Because your old one broke."

Bizarro smiled as he inspected the gift. "Bizarro am #1!" he exclaimed.

Green Lantern placed his hand on Superman's shoulder. "What have we got ourselves into?" he asked.

Wonder Woman arrived on the scene bringing news. "The Javelin is ready," she said. "Let's get going."

The team returned to their newly repaired ship and took off towards Bizarro's world.

CHAPTER 4

HOME AT LAST

"Me am finally home!" Bizarro shouted, jumping up and down. Each time his feet hit the floor, the Javelin rocked from side to side.

"Enough of the jumping," said Green Lantern. "I need to land this thing."

Superman looked out the cockpit window and was heartbroken by what he saw. What was once a beautiful, peaceful place had been turned into an empty wasteland. Its bright colours turned grey. Its plant life dead and its streams dried up completely. The team got out to view their new surroundings.

"What happened here?" Superman asked.

"New Bizarros ruin old Bizarro's home and steal his best friend. BIZARRO-KRYPTO!" Bizarro shouted into the sky. "Me am coming to find you!"

"Lower your voice. We'll need the element of surprise if we want to defeat our enemies," warned Wonder Woman.

"How many of these *bad* Bizarros are there altogether?" Supergirl asked.

"Hmmmmm," Bizarro said, scratching his head. He closed his eyes and mumbled to himself. He seemed to be counting. "Aha!" he exclaimed. Bizarro used his freeze vision to carve a number into the ground.

"One hundred?!" Green Lantern exclaimed. "Are you telling us *one hundred Bizarros* are wandering around out there?"

"Yes! But me am *#1!*" Bizarro said, showing off his new medallion.

Wonder Woman spotted a trio of approaching Bizarros. They were coming in fast. "So much for the element of surprise," she said. "I'll handle this."

Wonder Woman launched herself into the air as the first Bizarro swooped in, grabbing wildly at her legs. She gave him a swift kick to the gut that sent him flying in the opposite direction. The second Bizarro fired a blast of freeze vision. She deflected it back at him using her silver bracelets.

As the first two Bizarros regrouped, Wonder Woman decided to play a game with the third. She flew around in circles, knowing he would follow her. After a while, the third Bizarro became dizzy. That's when Wonder Woman lassoed the dazed clone.

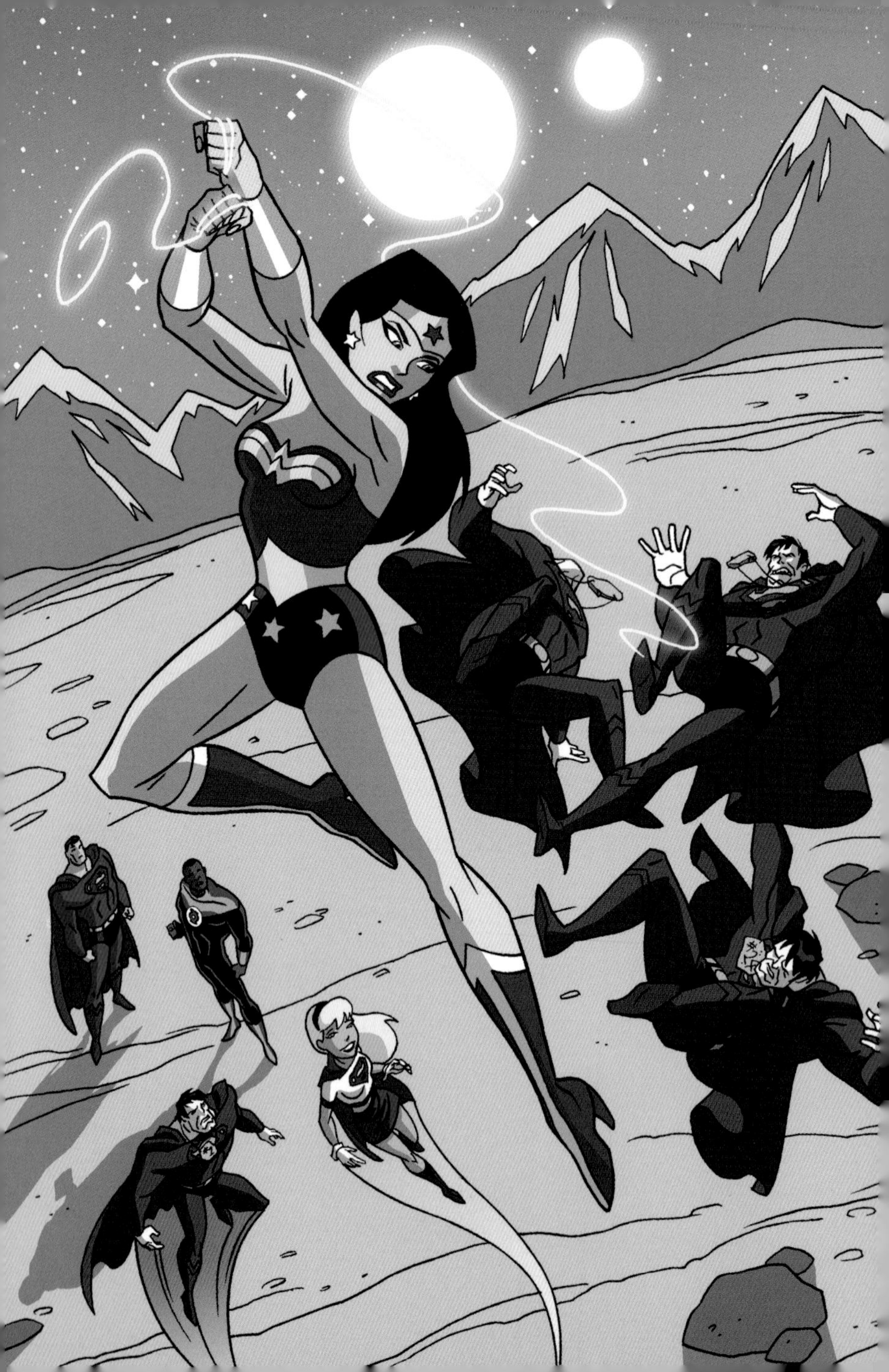

With a flick of the wrist, Wonder Woman swung the dazed clone at his two friends, knocking them all out at once. The trio of Bizarros fell from the sky, landing in a pile on the ground.

Supergirl was stunned by Wonder Woman's prowess in battle. "That was amazing," she said. "Can you teach *me* how to fight like that?"

"It would be my honour," said Wonder Woman. "But first we need a plan to take down the rest of these monsters."

"Finding them should be easy," Superman said. "But Batman suggested the flawed cloning technology made these clones deeply unstable. That makes our job more difficult."

"Let's see what's in that box he gave you," said Green Lantern. "We're in need of a secret weapon."

Superman took a deep breath, slowly opening the lid of the lead-lined box. Inside was a piece of glowing blue rock. "Blue Kryptonite. Of course. It's the only kind of Kryptonite that can hurt Bizarro," said the Man of Steel.

Bizarro #1 used his super-breath to blow the box out of Superman's hand and onto the ground. "You want to hurt Bizarro!" he screamed. "You not friend! You *enemy!*"

"Uh-oh," said Green Lantern.

Superman picked up the Blue Kryptonite and put it back in the box. "There's no need to be frightened. No one is going to use this on *you*. I'll put it away, okay? We're here to help," Superman explained.

Bizarro growled at Superman like an animal. He wasn't convinced.

"It's all right, Bizarro," Supergirl comforted. "I won't let anyone hurt you."

"We're losing time," reminded Wonder Woman. "Superman and I will round up the Bizarros. Green Lantern, you'll need to create something that can hold them all."

Green Lantern used his power ring to build a gigantic globe-like prison. "How about a hamster ball?" he asked.

"Works for me," Superman replied.

"With so many Bizarros out there, I'm going to need you all to guard my back. The last thing I need is to get attacked when I'm not looking," said Green Lantern.

"Green Lantern no worry. Me be bodyguard. Me protect you!" Bizarro said, slapping Green Lantern's back. "But who will find poor Bizarro-Krypto?" he asked.

Supergirl sheepishly raised her hand. "I could do it," she said.

After what had happened during their detour, Superman wasn't about to let Supergirl search for Bizarro-Krypto alone.

"I need to speak to you, Superman," Wonder Woman said. "In private."

The two heroes found a place close by where Wonder Woman made her case. "I understand your concerns about Supergirl. She made a mistake going off on her own. But you haven't put yourself in her shoes. You haven't considered her point of view."

"It's my job to watch out for her," said Superman. "If she wants to be a full-time Justice Leaguer, she needs to prove herself."

"She's proved herself many times before," Wonder Woman explained.

"The life we lead is dangerous," said Superman. "Supergirl is the only Kryptonian family I've got. I don't know what I'd do if I lost her."

"If you continue to hold her back, you won't have a choice in the matter," said Wonder Woman.

"Get ready, everyone!" Green Lantern shouted. "It's about to get crazy!"

A horde of angry Bizarros approached in the distance. Superman and Wonder Woman ended their conversation and rushed back to form a plan of action.

"Supergirl, fly above the terrain. Use your X-ray vision to find out where the Bizarros are holding Bizarro-Krypto, then retrieve him," said Superman. "Remember, the Bizarro's aren't very bright. Use that to your advantage."

Supergirl's eyes widened with excitement. "You got it!" she exclaimed, bounding into the sky.

"Everyone knows what to do. Superman and I will help get the Bizarros into the prison while Bizarro #1 makes sure Green Lantern isn't disturbed," Wonder Woman said. The unruly Bizarros were getting closer and the Justice League was ready to take them on.

* * *

Supergirl scanned the surrounding area but found nothing. Bizarro-Krypto was nowhere to be seen.

There must be too much lead in the atmosphere, she thought. *It's messing with my X-ray vision. Time to switch tactics.*

Supergirl used her super-hearing, hoping to pick up Bizarro-Krypto's heartbeat. The plan worked, and soon she tracked him down to a small cave on the side of a nearby mountain. There was just one problem. An angry Bizarro clone was guarding the entrance.

"Who am you?!" the clone grumbled.

"*I'm* here to take you down and rescue Bizarro-Krypto," said Supergirl. "Kindly step aside or I'll have to use force. Trust me, you won't like that."

"Me am Bizarro #45! The best of all Bizarros! Puny flying girl not stop me," the clone said, charging towards Supergirl like an angry bull. She dodged him with ease. Bizarro #45's hasty attack left the cave entrance wide open.

"Ha!" Supergirl laughed. "You're the worst security guard *ever.*" Before she could enter the cave, Bizarro #45 thundered into the rocks above it. He broke them apart, causing an avalanche that blocked the entrance completely.

"Now you not get inside. Bizarro #45 win!" the clone exclaimed.

That does present a minor problem, Supergirl thought. Then she remembered Superman's advice. She picked up a piece of rubble and showed it to Bizarro #45. "I bet you can't fetch this rock," Supergirl taunted.

"Ha, ha, ha!" Bizarro #45 cackled. "Me fetch *so good.* Prove flying girl wrong!"

Supergirl reared back and used her super-strength to throw the rock far, far away. Bizarro #45 took off after it like a puppy.

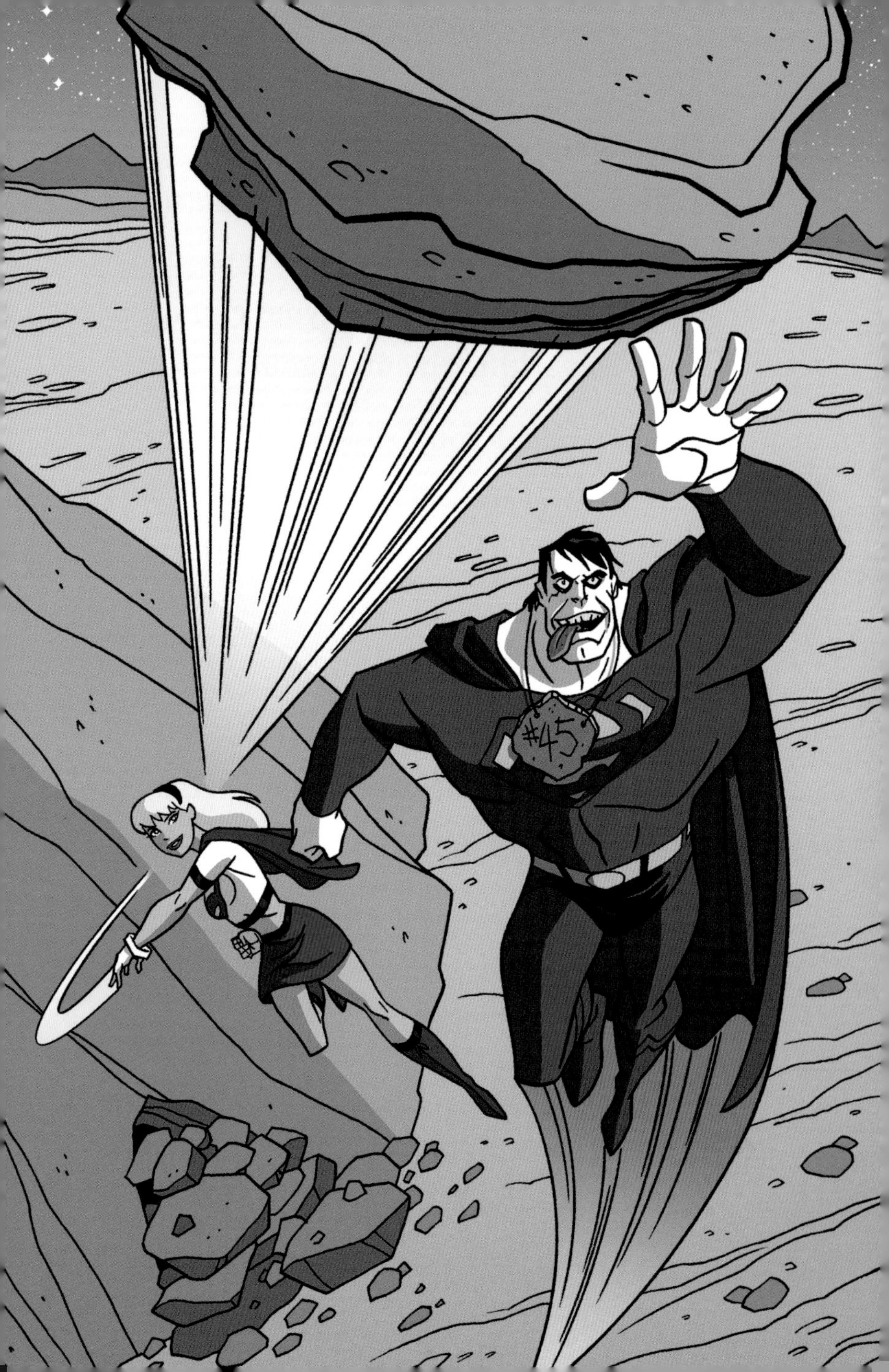
#45

"That should buy me a little time," Supergirl said. She began clearing boulders from the cave's entrance as fast as possible. Supergirl could hear Bizarro-Krypto's faint whimper deep within the mountain.

"I'm coming for you," she assured. "Don't worry." Supergirl worked faster, moving boulder after boulder. *I've got to hurry if I want to save Bizarro-Krypto before Bizarro #45 returns,* she thought.

It was already too late. Bizarro #45 was back and he wasn't pleased. He dropped the rock on the ground and slowly made his way towards the Girl of Steel.

"Flying girl try to *trick* Bizarro #45, but *me am smarter,*" he snarled. "You in big, big trouble now!"

CHAPTER 5

BATTLE OF THE BIZARROS

"This is beginning to annoy me," grunted Superman. He and Wonder Woman had been battling packs of wild Bizarros. The task was draining their energy. A rowdy Bizarro seized Superman from behind and wrestled him in mid-air. The Man of Steel quickly got the upper hand and threw the clone into the green prison.

"One moment the Bizarros are enraged, and the next minute they're distracted," Wonder Woman said. "It's like trying to herd an army of unruly toddlers."

"Sounds like they're a chip off the old block," Superman said, hurling a Bizarro clone through the air and into Green Lantern's prison. "How many more do we have to catch?"

Green Lantern strained to hold his construct together. The captive Bizarros scratched at it desperately, trying to escape.

"I'd say twenty or so Bizarros are still out there," Green Lantern said. "Hurry it up, would you? These guys aren't easy to hold."

Another swarm of Bizarros moved in on their location. They had a crazed look in their eyes. Bizarro #1 prepared to stand his ground. "Me have your back, Green Lantern," he declared.

"You not welcome here, Bizarro #1! This place only for Bizarros #2 to #100 now!" screamed a rude Bizarro bully.

"You not tell me what to do, Bizarro #18! Me am Bizarro #1. Me the best Bizarro there is!" exclaimed Bizarro #1.

One of the Bizarros battling Superman strongly disagreed. "No, *me* the best Bizarro there is!" he shouted, punching at the Man of Steel and missing.

"You both am wrong! *Me* am the best!" another Bizarro cried from inside Green Lantern's prison.

"If you so good then why you in prison?" Bizarro #1 asked.

Superman was at his wit's end. "Focus, Bizarro #1!" he exclaimed. The Man of Steel spun himself at super speed, creating a whirlwind that pushed his Bizarro attackers away. While they were winded, he scooped each of them up and threw them into Green Lantern's prison.

"Just a few more left. Hang in there, Green Lantern," Superman assured.

Wonder Woman spotted two naughty Bizarros trying to break into the Javelin. "No, you don't!" she said, hurling her lasso in their direction. She snagged them both and yanked them away from the ship. Wonder Woman gave her lasso a final tug that launched the Bizarros safely into the prison.

Suddenly Bizarro #1's ears caught the sound of a voice crying out in the distance.

"Now me *really* have to go!" Bizarro said. "Supergirl in trouble!" He took off like a shot in search of his friend, leaving Green Lantern open to attack. Bizarros were flying in from every direction.

"A little help over here would be nice," Green Lantern pleaded.

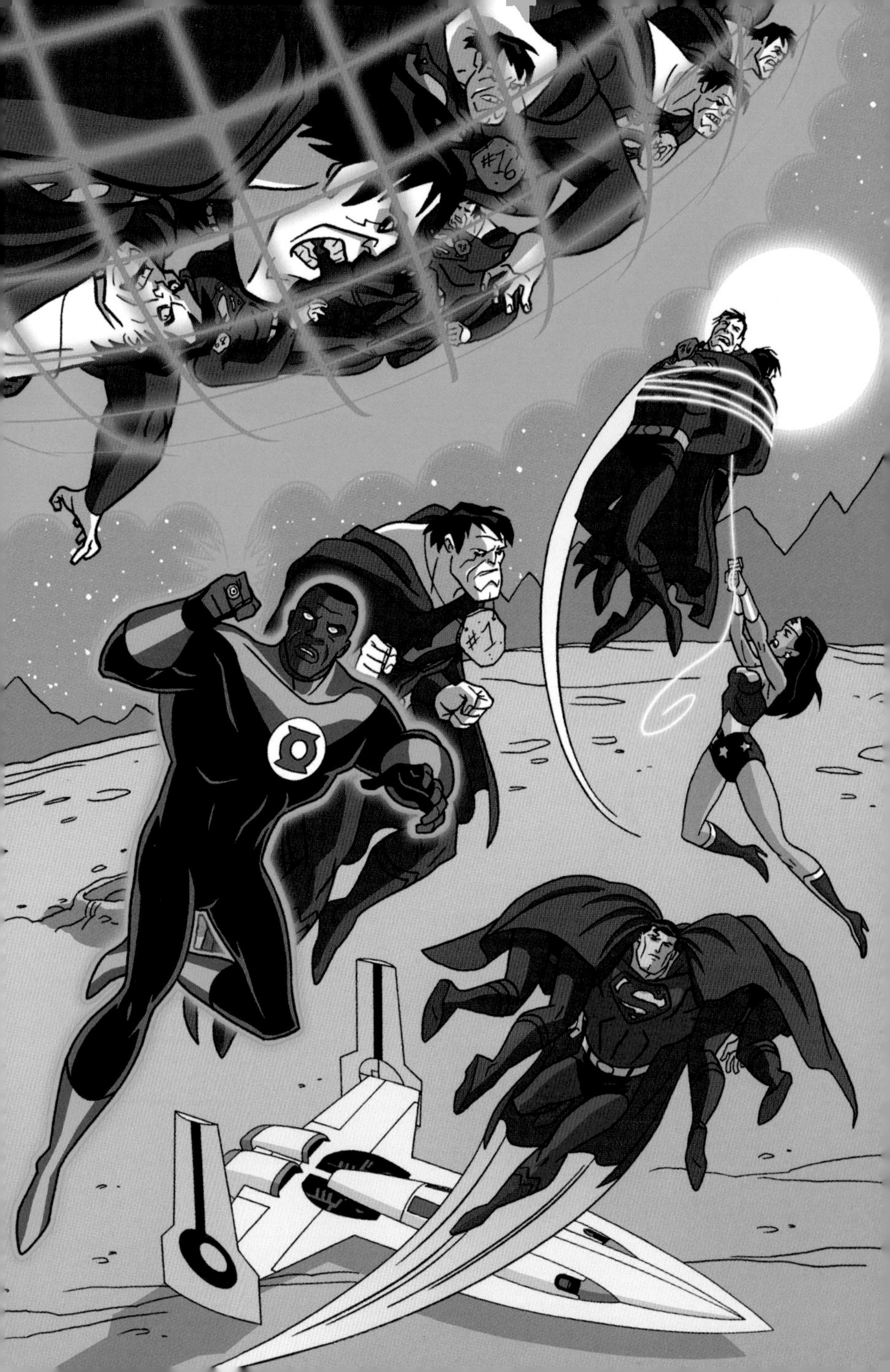
#16
#1

"Now that Bizarro #1 is gone, we can use Batman's secret weapon without hurting him," Superman said. He carefully removed the box of Blue Kryptonite from his belt, but a Bizarro plucked it out of his hands.

"Box am so ugly! Bizarro #72 had to have it. Me must keep it safe from harm," the clone said, flying off into the sky. Wonder Woman tackled him from behind, but he threw the box to a handful of other Bizarros on the ground.

"Protect ugly box, Bizarro #10!" Bizarro #72 shouted. "It am very important!"

Bizarro #10 was very curious about the box's contents. He couldn't help but see what was inside. He flipped open the lid and was bathed in the glow of Blue Kryptonite.

"Me feel so weak and sleepy. Want to go night-night," Bizarro #10 said.

The surrounding Bizarros watched with fright as their colleague collapsed.

"Simple and effective," Wonder Woman said. "Who's next?"

* * *

On the neighbouring mountainside, Bizarro #45 had Supergirl cornered. "Me not *dumb* like *other* Bizarros. Bizarro #45 going to *hurt* you," he declared. "Bye-bye, flying girl!"

"Hey, look! Over there!" Supergirl yelled.

THWACK! The Girl of Steel knocked Bizarro #45 off his feet with a blow. "The name is *Supergirl* and I'm not going *anywhere*," she said.

Bizarro #1 arrived and was excited to see his least favourite clone laying on the ground in defeat.

"Ha, ha, ha! Bizarro #45 think he *so clever,* but he just a dummy," Bizarro #1 taunted. "Dummy, dummy, dummy!"

"Me am not a dummy! You am dummy!" screeched Bizarro #45. He tackled Bizarro #1 and the two clones tussled on the ground.

This is my chance to save Bizarro-Krypto, Supergirl thought, *but the cave entrance is still littered with boulders. I don't have time to remove them all by hand.*

Supergirl spun in circles like a super drill, burrowing through the rubble and clearing it completely.

Bizarro-Krypto was chained up in the corner of the cave. Supergirl approached him with caution. She wasn't sure how he would react, seeing as she was a stranger.

GRRRRRRR!

"I'm not here to hurt you," she comforted. "I know I'm not your master, but he's busy at the moment. Be a good boy and maybe you'll get a treat?"

Bizarro-Krypto jumped wildly towards Supergirl but was stopped by his chain. *How am I going to do this?* she wondered.

Outside, Bizarro #1 and Bizarro #45 struggled to defeat one another, but neither was making any progress.

"You think you *best* Bizarro but that not true. Bizarro #45 only care about himself!" exclaimed Bizarro #1. "That make you *worst* Bizarro ever!"

"You make me *angriest* Bizarro ever, that am for sure!" yelled Bizarro #45. The villain grabbed Bizarro #1 in a tight squeeze. Bizarro #1 wriggled free and flipped Bizarro #45's cape completely over his head.

"Who turn out lights?!" asked Bizarro #45. "You know me am afraid of dark!"

"That keep you busy for a while," Bizarro #1 said. He headed into the cave where the sight of his best friend filled him with joy. "Bizarro-Krypto!" he exclaimed.

"He's not the *friendliest* thing I've ever met," said Supergirl.

"Bizarro-Krypto, be nice! Supergirl am friend!" said Bizarro #1. In an instant Bizarro-Krypto went from snarling to loving. Supergirl ripped off his chains and he ran towards Bizarro #1.

"My best friend!" Bizarro #1 shouted. Bizarro-Krypto jumped into his arms and began licking his face.

"Okay, that's gross," said Supergirl. "Hey, what happened to Bizarro #45?"

"Help! It am so dark in here!" Bizarro #45 said, running around in circles. He tripped on a pebble, stumbled into the mountainside and knocked himself out.

"That takes care of *that*," Supergirl said. "Let's get out of here." She picked up Bizarro #45, flung him over her shoulder, and took off with Bizarro #1 to meet the rest of the League. By the time they reunited, Superman and Wonder Woman had successfully contained the remaining wild Bizarros. They were ready to wrap things up.

Supergirl was about to throw Bizarro #45 into Green Lantern's prison ball when he suddenly grabbed her and put her in a headlock.

"Ha! Me fool you. Bizarro #45 play dead!" he exclaimed. "Heroes stay back or me hurt her *bad*."

Seeing Bizarro #45 harm Supergirl filled Bizarro #1 with rage. He snatched the Blue Kryptonite from Superman's grasp.

"What are you doing?!" Superman yelled.

"Bizarro save Supergirl!" yelled Bizarro #1. "Uh-oh. Me not feel so good now."

The Blue Kryptonite weakened Bizarro #1's body instantly. He clutched the glowing rock and pushed through the pain. He wasn't about to give up on his family.

"No! You cheat!" Bizarro #45 shouted. Bizarro #1 shoved the Blue Kryptonite in his enemy's face, causing him to loosen his grip. Supergirl swiftly slipped from Bizarro #45's grasp and hurled him into the prison ball.

Drained by the Blue Kryptonite, Bizarro #1 fell from the sky. Supergirl caught him and safely set him on the ground.

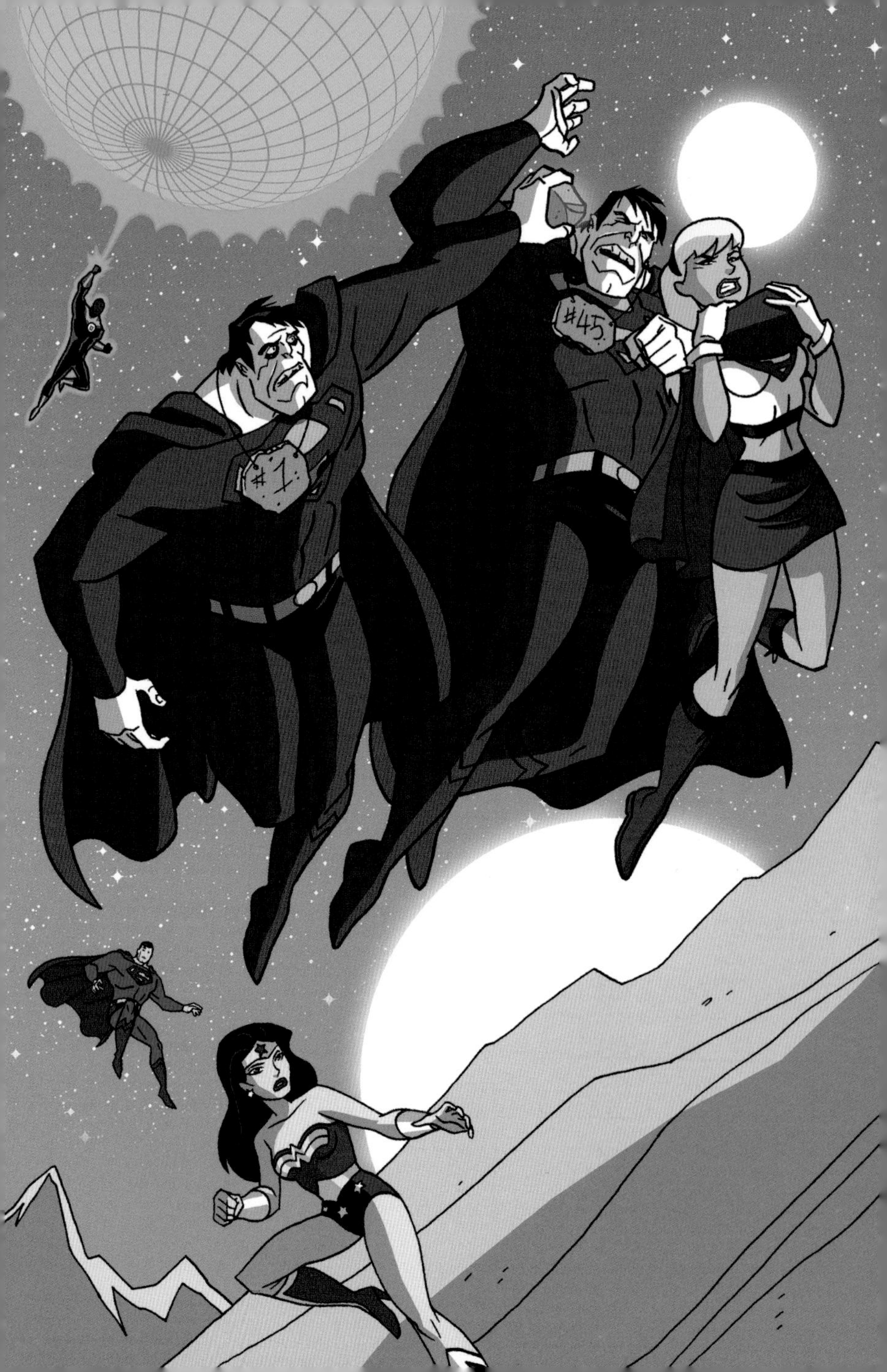
#1
#45

Superman retrieved the Blue Kryptonite and threw it into the sphere. The Bizarros scrambled in panic to avoid it. "That should keep them busy," he said. Then Green Lantern used his ring to seal the prison shut.

"Thank you, Bizarro," said Supergirl. "I owe you my life."

"It no problem. You *family*, Supergirl," Bizarro #1 said with a grin. "Me have one last thing to do."

Despite his weakened state, Bizarro grabbed the green ball and used his last bit of energy to launch it into space. The Justice Leaguers were impressed and confused.

"Are we sure that was the right move?" asked Green Lantern. "That construct will dissolve once it's outside this planet's orbit. What's stopping the Bizarros from coming back here or causing problems elsewhere."

"They'll keep travelling into deep space until they find a place to live. That will take a *very* long time considering this star system is uninhabited," Superman explained. "Plus, they don't have a great sense of direction."

"That why me make spaceship to find Justice League! Bizarro not so good at finding things on his own," said Bizarro #1. "Me need help sometimes."

"Nice work, Bizarro," Wonder Woman complimented.

"Bizarro am #1! Bizarro am #1!" he chanted.

"Nothing beats the original," Green Lantern said.

As the team prepared to leave, Bizarro pulled Supergirl aside to bid her a final farewell.

"You help Bizarro find his best friend. You am Bizarro's hero forever and ever and ever!" he said, giving her an awkward hug. "Will you come visit Bizarro again soon?"

Supergirl smiled. "Of course I will," she said. "Stay out of trouble, okay?"

Superman put his hand on Bizarro #1's shoulder to offer a final piece of advice. "What you did today took courage. You've got what it takes to be a hero, but you'll have to work for it. Keep it up," he advised. With that, the adventure to Bizarro's world ended.

As the Javelin took off into the sky, Supergirl wondered what life was really like for Bizarro. "It must be so hard for him. To be out here all alone, the last of his kind," she said. "I know he has a habit of turning on you, but there's something good inside him. We all saw it. I hope he finds some peace."

"Me too," Superman agreed. "I'm proud of you, Kara. You did a great job today."

"Thanks, cousin," said Supergirl. "That means a lot."

"I've been too hard on you lately. I'm sorry for that. Sometimes I forget you're not a girl anymore," Superman explained.

"Maybe I need to change my name to Superwoman one of these days," Supergirl joked.

"You're meant for something bigger. I've always known it, even though it hasn't always been easy for me to accept," said Superman. "You have a purpose to fulfill and I want to help you do that by offering you a *full-time* Justice League membership."

Supergirl's eyes lit up. "Oh *wow*," she said. "I don't know what to say."

"I hope you'll say *yes*," said Superman.

Supergirl had been waiting for this moment for a long time. But after everything that had happened, she wasn't sure that being a full-time Justice Leaguer was what she really wanted.

"I think I want to do my own thing, maybe start fresh somewhere new. I hear the weather in National City is nice this time of year," she said. "You've got my number if you need me. Give me a call and I'll be there in a flash."

"A greater destiny awaits you, sister," Wonder Woman said.

BEEP! BEEP! BEEP!

The Javelin received a call from the Watchtower. Green Lantern flipped a switch and Batman appeared on the monitor.

"I trust you've taken care of the Bizarro issue?" Batman asked.

"All's well that ends well," said Superman. "Thanks for the Blue Kryptonite."

"Don't mention it," Batman said. "Hurry home, would you? The Flash's Rogues have taken over Central City. We could really use your help."

"Copy that," said Green Lantern. "Buckle up, everyone. Full steam ahead." Then the Javelin's thrusters ignited as the ship blasted into the stars on a course for Earth.

〈 END 〉

{ TARGET: AT LARGE }

BIZARRO

Bizarro is an imperfect clone of Superman created by Lex Luthor. Although he was designed to destroy the Man of Steel, Bizarro fought Luthor's evil brainwashing. He rebelled against his master and made peace with Superman. Sadly, it didn't last. Bizarro fell in with a villainous crowd, and his mixed-up state of mind made him dangerous and unpredictable. Bizarro has all of Superman's powers and abilities, but he lacks the knowledge to use them correctly, though he's been known to surprise.

LEX LUTHOR

THE JOKER

CHEETAH

SINESTRO

CAPTAIN COLD

BLACK MANTA

AMAZO

GORILLA GRODD

STAR SAPPHIRE

BRAINIAC

DARKSEID

HARLEY QUINN

BIZARRO

THE SHADE

MONGUL

POISON IVY

MR. FREEZE

COPPERHEAD

ULTRA-
HUMANITE

CAPTAIN
BOOMERANG

SOLOMON GRUNDY

BLACK ADAM

DEADSHOT

CIRCE

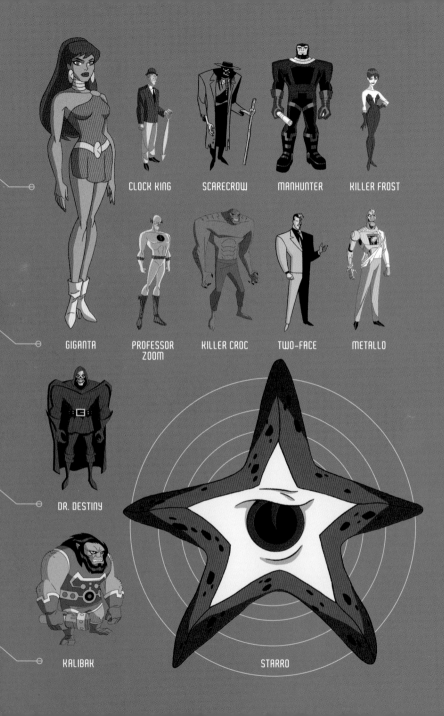

CLOCK KING

SCARECROW

MANHUNTER

KILLER FROST

GIGANTA

PROFESSOR ZOOM

KILLER CROC

TWO-FACE

METALLO

DR. DESTINY

KALIBAK

STARRO

STRENGTH IN NUMBERS

raintree
a Capstone company—publishers for children

GLOSSARY

affectionate loving

avalanche mass of snow, rocks, ice or soil that slides down a mountain slope

clone use an animal's cells to grow another identical animal

DNA material in cells that gives people their individual characteristics; DNA stands for deoxyribonucleic acid

duplicate exact copy

hologram image made by laser beams that looks three-dimensional

orbit path an object follows as it goes around the Sun or a planet

sphere round, solid shape like a football or a globe

technology use of science to do practical things, such as designing complex machines

tentacle long, arm-like body part some animals use to touch, grab or smell

thermal having to do with heat or holding in heat

1. If Supergirl becomes a full-time Justice League member, she'll have to take on new responsibilities. What responsibilities do you have? Compare your responsibilities to a friend's.

2. Wonder Woman is like a mentor to Supergirl. Do you have mentors who encourage you? What sort of good advice have they given you?

3. This book has ten illustrations. Which one is your favourite? Why?

1. Bizarro is influenced by the people around him. Who are the positive influences that surround you? Write about how they make you a better person.

2. If you had a clone, how would it behave and what would it like? Write a few paragraphs describing your clone and draw a picture to go with them.

3. Write a funny story about a Bizarro clone who gets lost on a strange and exciting planet. What does it see? What creatures does it meet? How does it get back home?

AUTHOR

BRANDON T. SNIDER has authored more than 75 books featuring pop culture icons such as Captain Picard, Transformers and the Muppets. Additionally, he's written books for Cartoon Network favourites such as *Adventure Time*, *Regular Show* and *Powerpuff Girls*. He's best known for the top-selling *DC Comics Ultimate Character Guide* and the award-winning *Dark Knight Manual*. Brandon lives in New York City and is a member of the Writer's Guild of America.

ILLUSTRATOR

TIM LEVINS is best known for his work on the Eisner Award-winning DC Comics series Batman: Gotham Adventures. Tim has illustrated other DC titles, such as *Justice League Adventures*, *Batgirl*, *Metal Men* and *Scooby-Doo*, and has also done work for Marvel Comics and Archie Comics. Tim enjoys life in Ontario, Canada, with his wife, son, dog and two horses.